W. R. Nettling

Uniform with this book
My Brother Sean · Sean's Red Bike

THE BODLEY HEAD

London Sydney Toronto

Text © Petronella Breinburg 1974   Illustrations © Errol Lloyd 1974   ISBN 0 370 02029 4
Printed in Great Britain for The Bodley Head Ltd, 9 Bow Street, London WC2E 7AL
by William Clowes Ltd, Beccles and London
First published 1974   Reprinted 1979, 1983

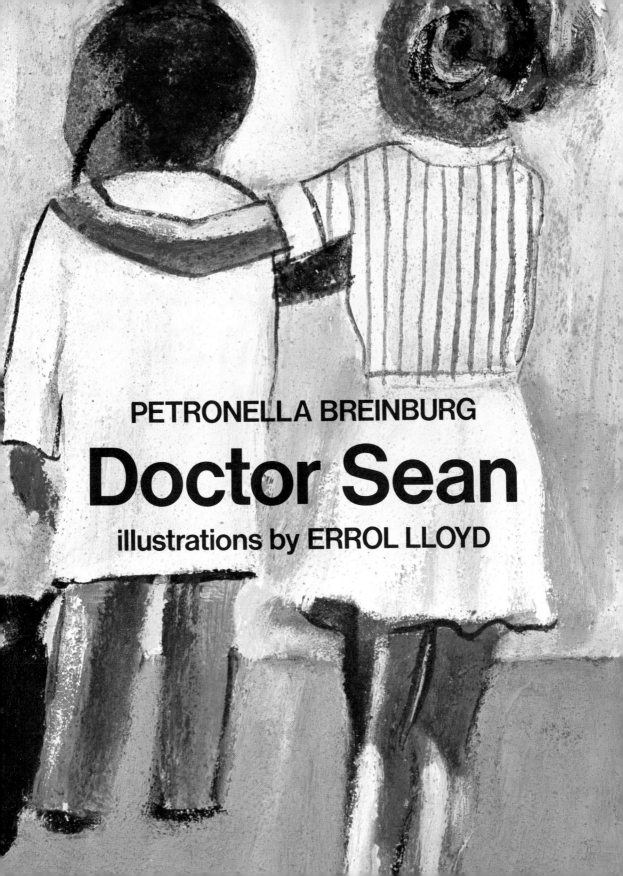

PETRONELLA BREINBURG

Doctor Sean

illustrations by ERROL LLOYD

It was Saturday, and before Mum went shopping she cleared the front room so that we could play.

"Don't make too much noise," said Mum, "because of the people who live downstairs."

"Yes, let's,"
said Sean.

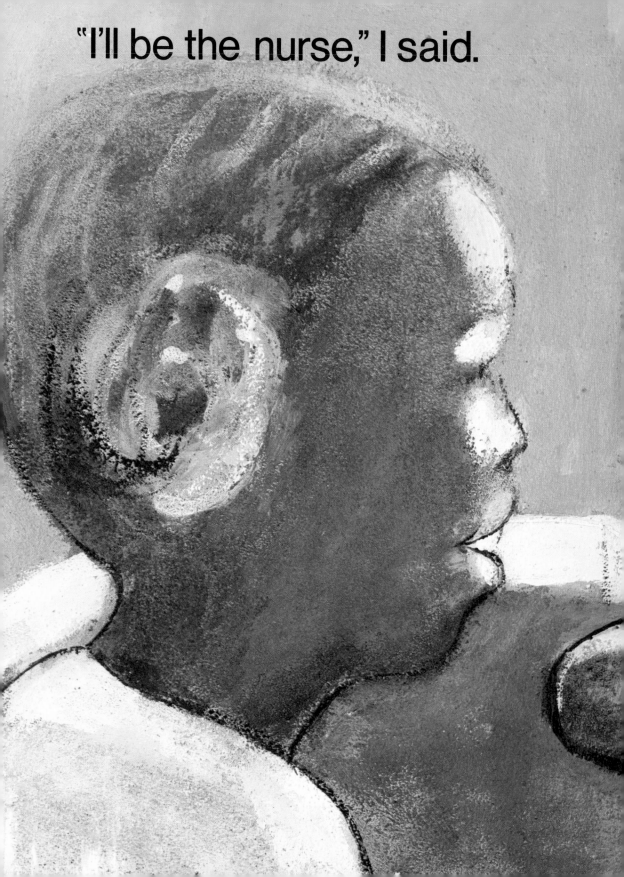

"I'll be the nurse," I said.

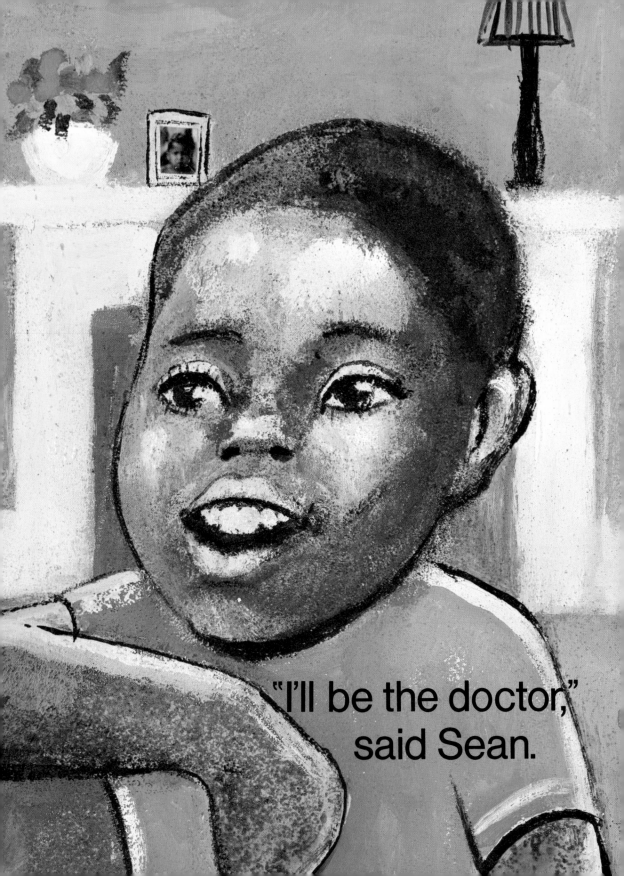

"I'll be the doctor,"
said Sean.

"And I'll be a sick child," said Josephine, and she started to groan.

We got the hospital
ready by pushing
the chairs aside.
A box became a bed
for Josephine's teddy,
and the Dutch doll
went into her own bed.

The others had to make do with a blanket on the floor.

We got out our hospital kit which we had been given last Christmas I put on my nurse's apron and my nurse's cap.

Then I picked up my bag.

I helped Sean to put on his doctor's gown. Round his neck he hung that thing doctors use to listen to people's chests.

And so the hospital began its day.
"A bandage for you, sir?" said
the doctor.

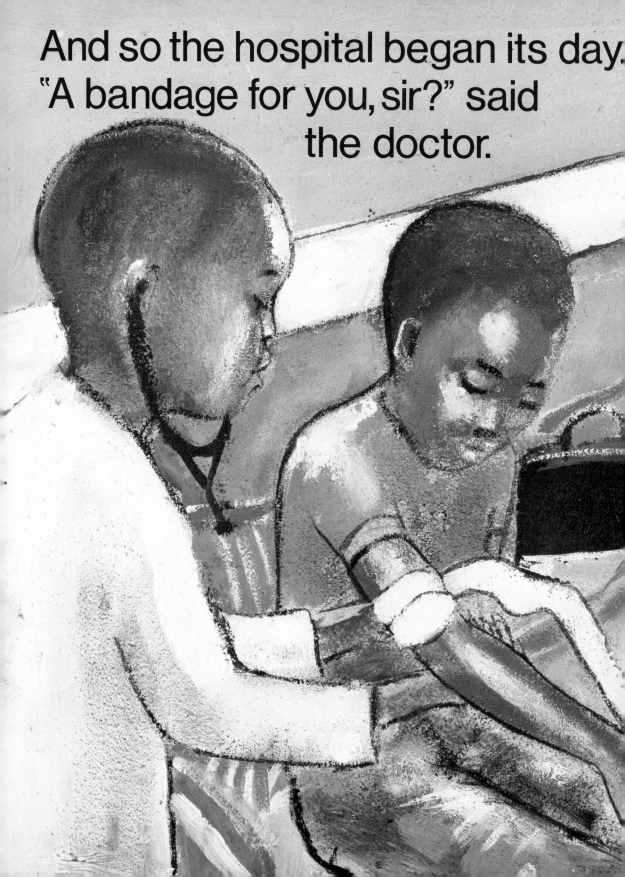

"Let me comb your hair,"
I said to Josephine.

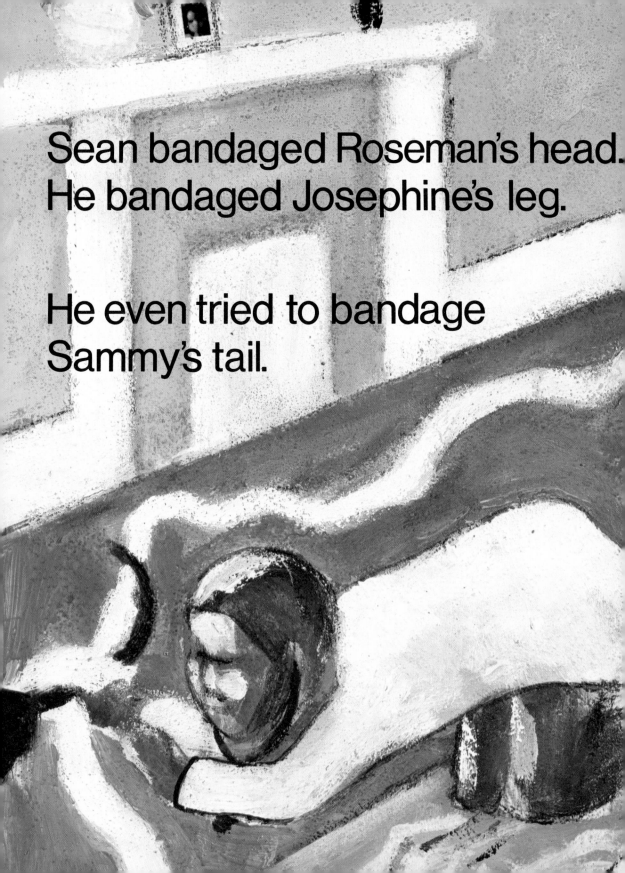

Sean bandaged Roseman's head.
He bandaged Josephine's leg.

He even tried to bandage
Sammy's tail.

But Sammy is only a cat,
so he struggled. Then
he ran like lightning.
Sean tried to grab
him – but he missed.

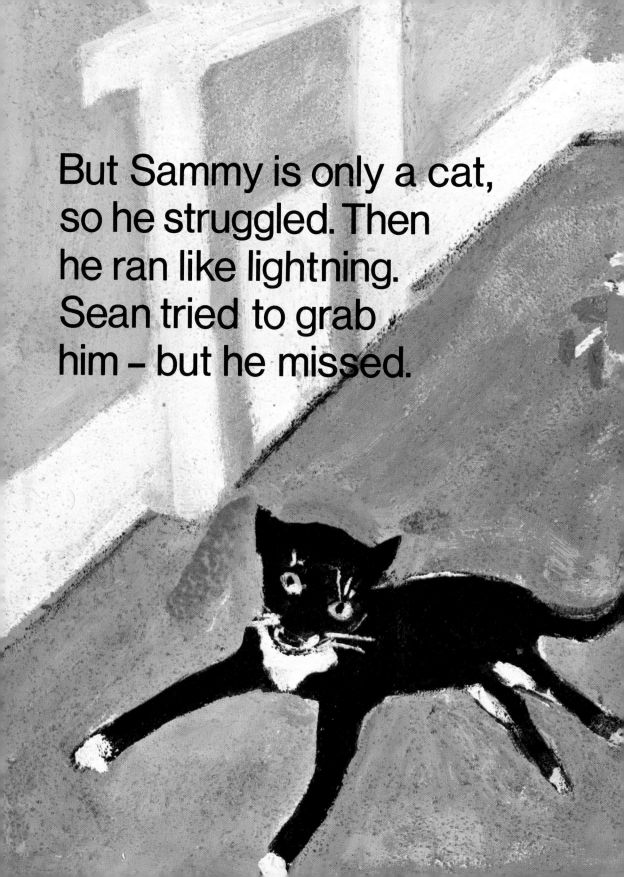

We played 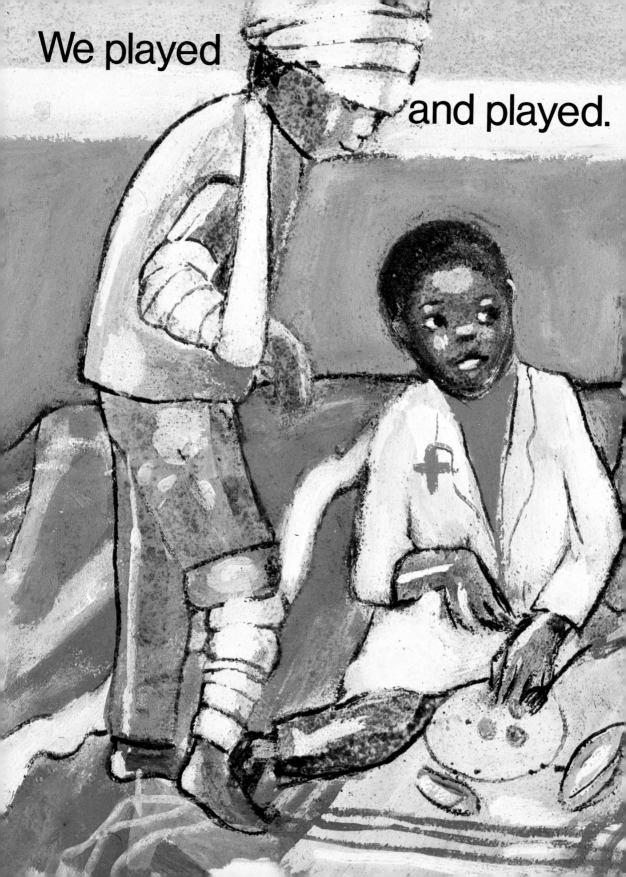 and played.

We made up pills from sliced bananas. And we played some more. Then Mum came home.

So our hospital day came to an end. We had to have dinner, you see!